W9-BFM-454

Weekly Reader Books presents

This

**READ
with
ME** ™

Book
Belongs To

Library of Congress Cataloging in Publication Data

Perle, Ruth Lerner.
  The fisherman and his wife, with Benjy and Bubbles.
  (Read with me series)
  Adapted from the Grimm brothers' Vom Fischer und seiner Frau.
  SUMMARY: A rhymed retelling of the classic tale of the fisherman and his greedy wife, with the addition of Benjy the bunny and Bubbles the cat.
  [1. Fairy tales. 2. Folklore—Germany. 3. Stories in rhyme] I. Horowitz, Susan, joint author. II. Maestro, Giulio. III. Grimm, Jakob Ludwig Karl, 1785-1863. Vom Fischer und seiner Frau. IV. Title. V. Series.
      PZ8.3.P423Fi   [398.2]   [E]   78-55629
        ISBN 0-03-044971-5

Weekly Reader Books' edition

The Fisherman and His Wife

with Benjy and Bubbles

Adapted by RUTH LERNER PERLE
and SUSAN HOROWITZ

Illustrated by GIULIO MAESTRO

Holt, Rinehart and Winston • New York

HR&W
Books

A kindly fisherman and his wife
Lived a poor and humble life.
The fisherman wanted nothing more
Than to spend his days beside the shore.
But his greedy wife and Bubbles the cat
Wished for this and wished for that.
She wished for silver, gold and silk;
And Bubbles wished for coconut milk.
But the fisherman never felt a lack
He was contented in their shack.
He fished all day with Benjy the bunny
And never felt the need for money.

A poor fisherman lived in a small shack.
His wife wanted to be rich.

Once, on a day that was sunny and fine,
The fisherman felt a tug on his line.
He pulled it out to have a look
And found a flounder on a hook!
The fish, all gold from tail to head,
Looked at the fisherman and said,
"I'm not a real fish; mark it well —
But a Prince under an evil spell.
Good Fisherman, oh, hear my cry!
Throw me back! Don't let me die."
The fisherman set the flounder free
And watched as it swam back to sea.

The fisherman hooked a magic fish.
"Please let me go," said the fish.
The fisherman let the magic fish go.

That evening, the fisherman heard his wife say,
"How many fish did you catch today?"
He said, "I pulled one from the sea—
All golden, and he talked to me!
He said he was a Prince, and so,
Of course, I let the poor thing go."

"You silly fool!" the wife replied.
  She stamped her foot and then she cried,
"That surely was a magic fish;
  He could grant you any wish!
  And since you saved his precious life,
  Demand a cottage for your wife."

The wife said, "Ask the magic fish
for a wish. Ask him for a little house."

Next day, she pushed him out the door
And Benjy followed, as before.
And though it was a sunny day,
The sea had turned all dull and gray.

The fisherman cried out to the sea,
"Oh, Golden Flounder, come to me!"
The flounder came and said, "I'll do
Almost anything for you."

The fisherman said, "My wife and cat
Wish for this and wish for that.
They would like a cottage, small,
Not too wide and not too tall.
It's just one wish—a little one!"
The fish replied, "Go home. It's done."

The magic fish said, "You will have
a little house."

When the fisherman came back,
He could not find his little shack.
In its place, a cottage stood
Surrounded by a pretty wood.
On every tree were plums to pluck
And on a pond, a goose and duck.

The fisherman plucked a plum and cried
"Now, Wife, you must be satisfied!
Aren't you glad I saved the fish?
He's granted you your dearest wish!"

The wife looked at the cottage, small,
And yawned and said, "This can't be all."

The wife had a fine little house.
"I want more!" she said.
"Now I must have a big house."

She sent her husband out the door
And said, "That fish must give me more!
Now don't come home to me until
I have a mansion on a hill."

The fisherman sighed and hurried back
To the sea—now bleak and black.
He called out to the stormy sea,
"Golden Flounder, come to me!"
The flounder came and said, "I'll do
Almost anything for you."

The fisherman cried, "She wants more still;
Give her a mansion on a hill.
It's one more wish—but only one!"
The fish replied, "Go home. It's done."

The fish said, "You will have a big house."

The man went home but did not find
The cottage he had left behind.
He walked along an avenue.
Up to a mansion with a view.
There was a lake, a waterfall,
And thirty swans—and that's not all—
A fountain spouting milk to drink,
A swimming pool and skating rink.
There was feasting near and far;
The cat was eating caviar!

The fisherman said, in a trembling voice,
"Now, Wife, you *surely* must rejoice!"
But she looked up at the waterfall
And yawned and said, "This can't be all!"

The wife had a big house.
"I want more!" she said. "Tell the fish
I must be King!"

Said the wife, "It's not enough!
I am made for better stuff!
I must be King! Go ask the fish.
And don't come back without my wish!"

The fisherman became afraid
When he heard the wish she made.
And yet he cried out to the sea,
"Oh, Golden Flounder, come to me!"

Again, the flounder said, "I'll do
Almost anything for you."
The man wailed, "Fish, there's one more thing;
Create a castle...crown her King.
I could not ask just anyone!"
The fish replied, "Go home. It's done!"

The fisherman went to see the fish again. "My wife wants to be King," he said.

When he came back, the fisherman spied
A giant castle, six miles wide!
It towered high above the trees,
Its banners blowing in the breeze!
He watched white stallions trot and prance
Amid great pomp and circumstance
While marching in a grand parade,
Were big brass bands in gold brocade
And Dukes and Duchesses and Earls
Brought gifts of rubies, jade and pearls.

And everywhere, in every place
Were pictures of his wife's proud face.

Now the wife had
a fine palace.

The wife sat on a glistening throne
Carved by hand of precious stone.
She wore a purple wig and crown,
An ermine cape and velvet gown.
And on her thumb, a signet ring
Was engraved: *Madame, the King.*

The maids and butlers in her service
Bowed and scraped and seemed quite nervous
As they watched the footmen kneel
And serve the cat a ten course meal.
And at all times, no need to mention,
An army stood at rapt attention!

The fisherman touched the royal ruff
And moaned, "At last, Wife, you have had enough!"
But she looked down the marble hall
And yawned and said, "This can't be all."

She was King.
"I want more!" said the wife. "I must
be Emperor, I must rule the Earth."

She shrieked, "My nature is too grand
To be the King of just one land.
I must be, to show my worth,
Emperor—of all the Earth!
Go quick, before my mood turns sour
And provide me with Imperial power."

The sea was foaming, fierce and dark;
(Benjy thought he saw a shark!)
The fisherman called out tearfully
"Golden Flounder, come to me!"
And the flounder said, "I'll do
Almost anything for you."
The poor man cried, "I plead again;
Make her Emperor of all men—
The greatest one beneath the sun."
The fish replied, "Go home. It's done."

The fisherman went to see the fish again.
"Make my wife Emperor," he cried.

When he came home, the fisherman saw
What no one ever saw before:
A mountain made of emerald
Towering high above the world.

Near the top, Kings, Queens and Jacks
Bore his wife upon their backs.
She wore a diamond studded robe
And twirled a sterling silver globe.
And standing guard upon the heights
There were a thousand and one knights!

The man wept, "Wife, you're greater than
Any woman, child or man!"
But she declared, "The Earth looks small;
I can't believe that this is all!"

Now, the wife was Emperor.
She ruled the Earth.
"I must have more!" she said.
"I must be Lord of the sea and sky."

She yawned and said, "I am so bored!
I'm not sufficiently adored.
I must command the sun to set
For if I don't, I'm not great yet.
I will control the sky and sea.
Lord of the Universe I shall be.
Go back down to the ocean shore
And tell the flounder I want more."

A bolt of lightning split the sea;
The man screamed, "Flounder, come to me!
It's for my wife I make this call.
Make her the Lord of one and all!"

The fisherman went to see the fish again. "Make my wife Lord of the sea and sky," he cried.

The fisherman was wracked with fear
As he watched the fish appear.
The flounder's eyes were streaked with red;
He leaped above the waves and said,
"Fisherman, I've given you
Cottages and castles, too,
Mountains, mansions with a view,
But this, I could not—would not—do!
I have fulfilled your every need;
Now, let there be an end to greed.

You will see, when you get back,
On the sand, your poor old shack.
There, together with your wife
You shall spend the days of your life."

The fish said, "Your wife is too greedy.
She cannot be Lord of the sea and sky.
Now she must live in the small shack again."

THE END